For my grandmother, Melvina,
who said I should write a book just like this one
and to whom I replied that I never would
—H. B.

For Arthur Rackham,
may you continue to inspire others
as you have me
—T. D.

Table of Contents

List of Full-Page Illustrations

Dear Reader,

Over the years that Tony and I have been
friends, we've shared the same childhood
fascination with faeries. We did not realize
the importance of that bond or how it might be
tested.

One day Tony and I—along with several other
authors—were doing a signing at a large bookstore.
When the signing was over, we lingered, helping
to stack books and chatting, until a clerk
approached us. He said that there had been a
letter left for us. When I inquired which one of
us, we were surprised by his answer.

"Both of you," he said.

The letter was exactly as reproduced on the
following page. Tony spent a long time just
staring at the photocopy that came with it.
Then, in a hushed voice, he wondered aloud about
the remainder of the manuscript. We hurriedly
wrote a note, tucked it back into the envelope,
and asked the clerk to deliver it to the Grace
children.

Not long after, a package arrived on my
doorstep, bound in red ribbon. A few days after
that, three children rang the bell and told me
this story.

What has happened since is hard to describe.
Tony and I have been plunged into a world we
never quite believed in. We now see that faeries
are far more than childhood stories. There is an
invisible world around us and we hope that you,
dear reader, will open your eyes to it.

Holly Black

Dear Mrs. Black and Mr. DiTerlizzi:

I know that a lot of people don't believe in faeries, but I do and I think that you do too. After I read your books, I told my brothers about you and we decided to write. We know about real faeries. In fact, we know a lot about them.

The page attached to this one is a photocopy from an old book we found in our attic. It isn't a great copy because we had some trouble with the copier. The book tells people how to identify faeries and how to protect themselves. Can you please give this book to your publisher? If you can, please put a letter in this envelope and give it back to the store. We will find a way to send the book. The normal mail is too dangerous.

We just want people to know about this. The stuff that has happened to us could happen to anyone.

Sincerely,

Mallory, Jared, and Simon Grace

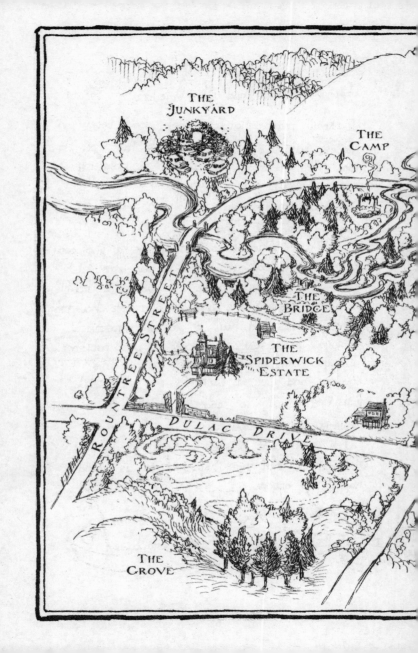

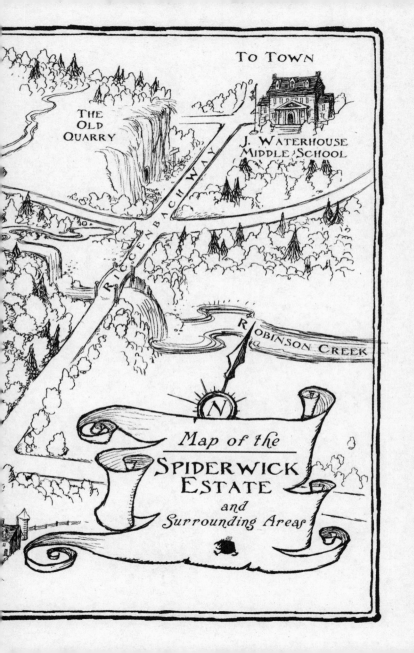

The place looked as bad as Jared felt.

Chapter One

IN WHICH More Than a Cat Goes Missing

The late bus dropped Jared Grace at the bottom of his street. From there it was an uphill climb to the dilapidated old house where his family was staying until his mother found something better or his crazy old aunt wanted it back. The red and gold leaves of the low-hanging trees around the gate made the gray shingles look forlorn. The place looked as bad as Jared felt.

He couldn't believe he'd had to stay after school already.

It wasn't like he didn't try to get along with

the other kids. He just wasn't good at it. Take today, for example. Sure, he'd been drawing a brownie while the teacher was talking, but he was still paying attention. More or less. And she didn't have to hold up his drawing in front of the whole class. After that, the kids wouldn't stop bothering him. Before he knew it, he was ripping some boy's notebook in half.

He'd hoped things would be *better* at this school. But since his parents' divorce, things had gone from bad to worse.

Jared walked into the kitchen. His twin, Simon, sat at the old farmhouse table with an untouched saucer of milk in front of him.

Simon looked up. "Have you seen Tibbs?"

"I just got home." Jared went to the fridge and took a swig of apple juice. It was so cold that it made his head hurt.

"Well, did you see him *outside*?" Simon

asked. "I've looked everywhere."

Jared shook his head. He didn't care about the stupid cat. She was just the newest member of Simon's menagerie. One more animal wanting to be petted or fed, or jumping on his lap when he was busy.

Jared didn't know why he and Simon were so different. In movies, identical twins got cool powers like reading each other's minds with a look. It figured that the most real-life twins could do was wear the same-size pants.

Their sister, Mallory, thundered down the stairs, lugging a large bag. The hilts of fencing swords stuck out from one end.

"Hey, good job getting detention, nutcase." Mallory slung the bag over her shoulder and walked toward the back door. "At least this time, no one's nose got broken."

"Don't tell Mom, okay, Mal?" Jared pleaded.

"Whatever. She's going to find out sooner or later." Mallory shrugged and headed out onto the lawn. Clearly this new fencing team was even more competitive than the last. Mallory had taken to practicing at every spare moment. It bordered on obsessive.

"Hey, good job getting detention, nutcase."

"I'm going to Arthur's library," Jared said, and started up the stairs.

"But you have to help me find Tibbs. I waited for you to get home so you could help."

"I don't *have* to do anything." Jared took the stairs two at a time.

In the upstairs hall he opened the linen closet and went inside. Behind the stacks of mothball-packed, yellowed sheets was the door to the house's secret room.

It was dim, lit faintly by a single window, and had the musty smell of old dust. The walls were lined with crumbling books. A massive desk covered in old papers and glass jars dominated one side of the room. Great-Great-Uncle Arthur's secret library. Jared's favorite place.

He glanced back at the painting that hung next to the entrance. A portrait of Arthur Spiderwick peered down at him with small eyes

half hidden behind tiny, round glasses. Arthur
didn't look that old, but he had a pinched mouth
and he seemed stuffy. He certainly didn't seem
like someone who would believe in faeries.

Opening the first drawer on the left-hand side of the desk, Jared tugged free a cloth-wrapped book: *Arthur Spiderwick's Field Guide to the Fantastical World Around You.* He'd only found it a few weeks before, but already Jared had come to think of it as *his.* He kept it with him most of the time, sometimes even sleeping with it under his pillow. He would have even brought it to school, but he was afraid someone would take it from him.

There was a faint sound inside the wall.

"Thimbletack?" Jared called softly.

He could never be sure when the house brownie was around.

Jared put the book down next to his latest project—a portrait of his dad. No one, not even Simon, knew that Jared had been practicing drawing. He wasn't very good—in fact, he was awful. But the Guide was for recording stuff, and to record well, he was going to have to learn to draw. Still, after today's humiliation, he didn't feel much like bothering. To be honest, he felt like tearing the picture of his father to pieces.

"There is a fell smell in the air," said a voice close to Jared's ear. "Best take care."

He whirled around to see a small nutbrown man dressed in a doll-size shirt and pants made from a dress sock. He was standing on one of the bookshelves at Jared's eye level, holding on to a piece of thread. At the top of the shelf, Jared could see the glint of a silver needle that the brownie had used to rappel down with.

"Thimbletack," Jared said, "what's wrong?"

"Could be trouble, could be nought. Whatever it is, it's what you wrought."

"What?"

"You kept the book despite my advice. Sooner or later there'll be a price."

"You always say that," said Jared. "What about the price for the sock you cut up to make your outfit? Don't tell me that was Aunt Lucinda's."

Thimbletack's eyes flashed. "Do not laugh, not today. You will learn to fear the fey."

Jared sighed and walked to the window. The last thing he needed was more trouble. Below, he could see the whole backyard. Mallory was close to the carriage house, stabbing at the air with her foil. Further out, near the broken-down plank fence that separated the yard from the nearby forest, Simon stood, hands cupped, probably calling for that stupid cat. Beyond that, thick trees obscured Jared's view. Downhill, in the distance, a highway cut through the woods, looking like a black snake in tall grass.

Thimbletack grabbed
hold of the thread and
swung over to the
window ledge. He
started to speak,
then just stared
outside. Finally
he seemed to get
his voice back.
"Goblins in the
wood. Doesn't look
good. My warning
comes too late. There's
no help for your fate."

"Where?"

"By the fence. Have you no sense?"

Jared squinted and looked in the direction
the brownie indicated. There was Simon, standing very still and staring at the grass in an odd

11

way. Jared watched in horror as his brother started to struggle. Simon twisted and struck out, but there was nothing there.

"Simon!" Jared tried to force the window open, but it was nailed shut. He pounded on the glass.

Then Simon fell to the ground, still fighting some invisible foe. A moment later, he disappeared.

"I don't see anything!" he shouted at Thimbletack. "What is going on?"

Thimbletack's black eyes gleamed. "I had forgotten, your eyes are rotten. But there is a way, if you do what I say."

"You're talking about the Sight, aren't you?"

The brownie nodded.

"But how come I can see you and not the goblins?"

"We can choose to show what we want you to know."

Jared grabbed the Guide and ruffled through pages he knew nearly by heart: sketches, watercolor illustrations, and notes in his uncle's scratchy handwriting.

"Here," Jared said.

The little brownie leapt from the ledge to the desk.

The page beneath Jared's fingers showed different ways to get the Sight. He scanned quickly. "'Red hair. Being the seventh son of a seventh son. Faerie bathwater'?" He stopped at the last and looked up at Thimbletack, but the little brownie was pointing excitedly down the page. The illustration showed it clearly, a stone with a hole through the middle, like a ring.

"With the lens of stone, you can see what's

The little brownie was pointing excitedly.

not shown." With that, Thimbletack jumped from the desk. He skittered across the floor toward the door to the linen closet.

"We don't have time to look for rocks," Jared yelled, but what could he do except follow?

It smelled of gasoline and mildew.

Chapter Two

IN WHICH Several Things Are Taken, Including a Test

Thimbletack sprinted across the lawn, hopping from shadow to shadow. Mallory was still fencing against the wall of the old carriage house, her back to where Simon had been.

Jared walked up behind her and tugged the headphones off her ears by the cord.

She turned, foil pointing at his chest. "What?"

"Simon's been grabbed by goblins!"

Mallory's eyes narrowed. She looked around the lawn. "Goblins?"

"Must make haste." Thimbletack's voice was as shrill as a bird's. "No time to waste."

"Come on." Jared gestured toward the carriage house where the little brownie was waiting. "Before they get us."

"SIMON!" Mallory shouted.

"Shut up." Jared took her arm and yanked her into the carriage house, closing the door after them. "They're going to hear you."

"Who is going to hear me?" Mallory demanded. *"Goblins?"*

Jared ignored her.

Neither one of them had been inside the building before. It smelled of gasoline and mildew. A tarp covered an old black car. Shelves lined the walls, cluttered with metal tins and mason jars half-filled with brown and yellow liquids. There were even stalls where horses must have been stabled long ago. A stack of boxes and leather trunks occupied one corner.

Thimbletack hopped up on a can of paint and pointed toward the boxes. "Hurry! Hurry! If they come, we must scurry!"

"If Simon got grabbed by goblins, why are we rooting through garbage?" Mallory asked.

"Here," Jared said, holding out the book and pointing to the picture of the stone. "We're looking for *this*."

"Oh, great," she said. "It'll be so easy to find in this mess."

"Just hurry," said Jared.

The first trunk contained a saddle, a few bridles, some combs, and other equipment for taking care of horses. Simon would have been fascinated. Jared and Mallory opened the next box together. It was full of old, rusted tools. Then they found a few boxes stuffed with tableware wrapped in dirty towels.

"Aunt Lucinda must have never thrown out anything," Jared said.

"Here's another one." Mallory sighed as she dragged a small wooden crate over to her brother. The top slid open in a dusty groove, revealing wadded up newspapers.

"Look how old these are," Mallory said. "This one says 1910."

"I didn't even think there were newspapers in 1910," said Jared.

Inside each crumpled piece of paper was a different item. Jared unrolled one to discover a pair of metal binoculars. In another he found a magnifying glass. The print below it was made huge. "This one's from 1927. They're all different."

Jared picked up another page. "'Girl drowns in empty well.' Weird."

"Hey, look at this." Mallory straightened one of the sheets. "1885. 'Local boy lost.' Says he was eaten by a bear. Look at the surviving brother's name! 'Arthur Spiderwick.'"

"There it is! This is his!" Thimbletack said, climbing into the box. When he resurfaced, he held the strangest eyepiece Jared had ever seen.

It covered only a single eye and attached to

The strangest eyepiece

the face with an adjustable nose clip as well as two leather straps and a chain. Backed in stiff, brown leather, four metal clamps waited to hold a lens of some kind. But the strangest thing about the device was the series of magnifying lenses on movable metal arms.

Thimbletack let Jared take the eyepiece and turn it over in his hands. Then he took a smooth stone with a hole through the center from behind his back.

"The lens of stone." Jared reached for it.

Thimbletack stepped back. "Here you must prove yourself or get nothing from this elf."

Jared stared in horror. "We don't have time for games."

"Time or not, you must tell if you will use this stone well."

"I only need it to find Simon," Jared said. "I'll give it right back."

Thimbletack cocked an eyebrow.

Jared tried again. "I promise that I won't let anyone use it—except Mallory—and, well, Simon. Come on! You're the one that suggested the stone in the first place."

"A human boy is like a snake. His promises are easy to break."

Jared's eyes narrowed. He could feel the frustration and anger rising up in him. His hands curled into fists. "Give me the stone."

Thimbletack said nothing.

"Give it to me."

"Jared?" Mallory cautioned.

But Jared barely heard her. There was a roaring in his ears as he reached out and grabbed hold of Thimbletack. The little brownie squirmed in his grasp, abruptly changing shape into a lizard, a rat that bit Jared's hand, then a slippery eel that flailed wetly. Jared was bigger, though, and he held fast. Finally, the stone dropped free, hitting the floor with a clatter. Jared covered it with his foot before he let

Thimbletack go. The brownie disappeared as Jared picked up the stone.

"Maybe you shouldn't have done that," said Mallory.

"I don't care." Jared put his bitten finger in his mouth. "We have to find Simon."

"Does that thing work?" Mallory asked.

"Let's see." Jared held the stone up to his eye and looked out the window.

"They're headed right for us."

Chapter Three

IN WHICH Mallory Finally Gets to Put Her Rapier to Good Use

Through the small hole in the stone, Jared saw goblins. There were five of them, all with faces like frogs' and eyes that were dead white with no pupil at all. Hairless, cat-like ears stuck up from their heads, and their teeth were pieces of shattered glass and small, jagged rocks. Their green, bloated bodies moved swiftly over the lawn. One held a stained sack while the rest scented the air like dogs, moving in the direction of the carriage house. Jared backed away from the window, almost tripping on an old bucket.

"They're headed right for us," he whispered, ducking down.

Mallory gripped her foil more tightly, knuckles white. "What about Simon?"

"I didn't see him."

She lifted up her head and peered outside. "I don't see *anything*," she said.

Jared crouched down with the stone clutched in his palm. He could hear the goblins outside, grunting and shuffling as they got closer. He didn't dare look through the stone again.

Then Jared heard the sound of old wood snapping.

A rock hit one of the windows.

"They're coming," Jared said. He shoved the Guide into his backpack, not bothering to buckle it.

"Coming?" Mallory replied. "I think they're here."

Claws scraped at the side of the barn and little barks came from beneath the window. Jared's stomach turned to lead. He couldn't move.

"We have to do something," he whispered.

"We're going to have to make a run for the house," Mallory whispered back.

"We can't," Jared said. The memory of the goblins' jagged teeth and claws wouldn't leave him.

"A couple more planks and they'll be inside."

He nodded numbly, steeling himself to rise. Fumbling, he tried to fit the stone into the eyepiece and attach it to his head. The clip pinched his nose.

"On my mark," said Mallory. "One. Two. Three. Go!"

She opened the door and they both sprinted toward the house. Goblins hurtled after them. Clawed hands caught at Jared's clothes. He wrenched free and ran on.

Mallory was faster. She was almost to the door of the house when a goblin caught the back of Jared's shirt and pulled hard. He went down on his stomach in the grass. The stone flew out of the monocle. He dug his fingers into the dirt, holding on as much as he could, but he was being dragged backward.

He could feel the clasps on his pack loosening, and he screamed.

Mallory turned. Instead of running on toward the house, she started running back to him. Her fencing sword was still in her hand, but there was no way she could know what she was up against.

GOBLIN

He was being dragged backward.

"Mallory!" Jared shouted. "No! Run away!"

At least one goblin must have gone past him, because he saw Mallory's arm jerk and heard her cry out. Red lines appeared where nails scraped her. The headphones were ripped free from her neck. She spun and lashed out with the rapier, dealing a stinging blow to the air. It didn't seem like she had hit anything. She swung the sword in an arc, but again, nothing.

Jared kicked out hard with one of his legs, striking something solid. He felt the grip that held him slip, and he pulled himself forward, yanking his backpack out of their grasp. The contents spilled out and Jared was barely able to snatch up the Guide in time. Reaching around in the grass, he picked up the stone and scrambled to where Mallory was. Then he brought the stone to his eye and looked.

"Six o'clock," he shouted, and Mallory whirled, striking in that direction, catching a goblin across the ear. It howled. Rapier blades didn't have points but they sure stung when they hit.

"Shorter, they're shorter." Jared managed to pull himself to his feet so that he was standing with his back against Mallory's. All five goblins were circling them.

One lunged from the right. "Three o'clock," Jared shouted.

Mallory knocked the goblin to the ground easily.

"Twelve o'clock! Nine o'clock! Seven o'clock!" They were rushing all at once, and Jared didn't think Mallory could possibly manage. He hefted the field guide and swung it as hard as he could at the nearest goblin.

Thwack! The book hit the goblin hard enough to send it sprawling backward.

All five goblins were circling them.

Mallory had knocked down two more with hard blows. Now they circled more warily, gnashing teeth of glass and stone.

There was a strange call, like a cross between a bark and a whistle.

At that sound, the goblins retreated one by one into the woods.

Jared collapsed onto the grass. His side hurt and he was out of breath.

"They're gone," Jared said. He held out the stone to Mallory. "Look."

Mallory sat down next to him and held it up to her eye. "I don't see anything, but I didn't see anything a minute ago either."

"They still might come back." Jared rolled over and opened the Guide, flipping through the pages quickly. "Read this."

"'Goblins travel in roving bands looking for trouble.'" Mallory scowled at the words. "And look, Jared—'Cats and dogs missing is a sign that goblins are in the area.'"

They exchanged a glance. "Tibbs," Jared said with a shudder.

Mallory read on. "'Goblins are born without teeth and so find substitutes, such as the fangs of animals, sharp rocks, and pieces of glass.'"

"But it doesn't say anything about how to stop them," said Jared. "Or where they might have taken Simon."

Mallory didn't look up from the page.

Jared tried to keep his mind from imagining what the goblins might want with Simon. It seemed pretty obvious to him what they did with the cats and dogs, but he didn't want to believe that his brother could be . . . could be *eaten*. His gaze fell on the illustration of those horrible teeth.

Surely not. Surely there was some other explanation.

Mallory took a deep breath and pointed to the illustration. "It's going to be dark soon, and with eyes like that, they probably have better night vision than we do."

That was pretty smart. Jared resolved to write a note in the Guide about it when they got Simon back. He took off the eyepiece and slid the stone into place again, but the clamps were too loose to hold it.

"It doesn't work," Jared said.

"You have to adjust it," said Mallory. "We need a screwdriver or something."

Jared took a pocketknife from the back pocket of his pants. It had a screwdriver, a little knife, a magnifying glass, a file, bent scissors, and a place where there had once been a toothpick. Screwing down the clamps carefully, he fitted the stone into place.

"Here, let me tie it on your head right." Mallory knotted the leather straps until the monocle-apparatus was on tight. Jared had to squint a little to see properly, but it was much better than before.

"Take this," Mallory said, and handed him a practice rapier. The end wasn't pointed,

Time to find Simon

though, so he wasn't sure how much real damage it could do.

Still, it felt better to be armed. Tucking the Guide into his backpack, tightening the straps, and holding the sword in front of him, Jared started back down the hill into the darkening woods.

It was time to find Simon.

The air was different.

Chapter Four

IN WHICH Jared and Mallory Find Many Things, but Not What They're Looking For

Stepping into the woods, Jared felt a slight chill. The air was different, full of the smell of green things and fresh dirt, but the light was murky. He and Mallory stepped through tangles of jewelweed and past thin trees heaped with vines. Somewhere above them a bird started calling, making a harsh sound like an alarm. Beneath their footsteps, the ground was slick with moss. Twigs snapped as they passed and Jared heard the distant sound of water.

45

There was a streak of brown, and a small owl settled on a low branch. Its head cocked toward them as it bit into the small, limp mouse in its claw.

Mallory pushed through a knot of bushes, and Jared followed. Tiny burrs caught on his clothes and in his hair. They sidled around the crumbling trunk of a fallen tree swarming with black ants.

There was something different about his vision with the stone in place. Everything was brighter and more clear. But there was something else, too. Things moved in the grass, in the trees, things he couldn't quite see but was aware of for the first time. Faces made of bark and rock and moss that he only saw for an instant. It was as though the whole of the forest was alive.

"There." Mallory fingered a broken branch

and pointed to where clumps of ferns had been trampled. "That's the way they went."

They followed the trail of smashed weeds and snapped branches until they came to a stream. By then the woods had grown more shadowed, and the twilight sounds had increased. A cloud of gnats settled on them for a moment, then blew out toward the water.

"What do we do now?" Mallory asked. "Can you see anything?"

Jared squinted through the eyepiece and shook his head. "Let's just follow the stream. The trail has to pick up again."

They walked on through the forest.

"Mallory," Jared whispered, pointing at a huge oak tree. Tiny green and brown creatures were perched on a branch. Their wings resembled leaves, but their faces seemed almost human. Instead of hair, grass and flower buds grew from their tiny heads.

"What are you looking at?" Mallory raised her rapier and took two steps backward.

Jared shook his head slightly. "Sprites . . . I think."

"Why do you have that stupid expression on your face?"

"They're just . . ." He couldn't quite explain. He extended his hand, palm up, and stared in amazement as one of the creatures alighted on his finger. Soft feet tickled his skin as the tiny faerie blinked up at him with black eyes.

"Jared," Mallory said impatiently.

At the sound of her voice, the sprite jumped into the air. Jared watched as it spiraled upward into the leaves above.

The patches of sunlight filtering through the trees became tinged with orange. Up ahead,

the stream widened where it ran under the remains of a stone bridge.

Jared could feel his skin prickle as they got closer to the rubble, but there was no sign of goblins. The stream was very wide, almost

One alighted on his finger.

twenty feet across, and there was a darkness in the middle that seemed to speak of deep water.

Jared heard a distant sound like metal grating against metal.

Mallory stopped, looked across the water, and raised her head. "Did you hear that?"

"Could it be Simon?" Jared asked. He hoped it wasn't. It didn't sound human at all.

"I don't know," Mallory said, "but whatever it was, it's got something to do with those goblins. Come on!" With that, Mallory bounded in the direction of the noise.

"Don't go in there, Mallory," Jared said. "It's too deep."

"Don't be a baby," she said, and waded into the stream. She made two long strides and then dropped as though she had stepped off the edge of a cliff. Dark green water closed over her head.

Jared lunged forward. Dropping his rapier onto the bank, he plunged his hand into icy cold water. His sister bobbed to the surface, sputtering. She grabbed for his arm.

He had pulled her halfway onto the bank when something began to surface behind her. At first it seemed like a hill rising from the water, stony and covered in moss. Then a head emerged, the deep green of rotten river grass, with small black eyes, a nose that was gnarled like a branch, and a mouth full of cracked teeth. A hand reached toward them. Its fingers were as long as roots, and its nails were black with murk. Jared breathed in the stench of the bottom of the pool, putrid leaves, and old, old mud.

He screamed. His mind went completely blank. He couldn't move.

Mallory pulled herself the rest of the way onto the bank and looked over her shoulder.

Something began to surface.

TROLL

"What is it? What do you see?"

At her voice, Jared snapped into moving and stumbled wood-enly away from the stream, tugging her along with him. "Troll," he gasped.

The creature lunged after them. Long fingers dragged through the grass just short of where they were.

Then the creature howled and Jared looked back, but he couldn't see what had happened. It felt toward them again but jerked away when one long finger fell into a beam of light. The monster bellowed.

"The sun," Jared said. "It got burned by the sun."

"There's not much sun left," Mallory replied. "Let's go."

"Waaait," the monster whispered. Its voice was soft.

Yellow eyes regarded them steadily. "Cooome baaack. I haaave something for youuu." The troll extended a closed hand as though something might indeed be clutched in its palm.

"Jared, come on." Mallory's voice was almost pleading. "I can't see what you're talking to."

"Have you seen my brother?" Jared asked.

"Perhaaaps. I heard something a tiiime ago, but it was bright, too bright to look."

"That was him! It must have been. Where did they go?"

The head swung toward the remnants of the

bridge and then looked back at Jared. "Cooome closer and I will tell you."

Jared took a step back. "No way."

"Aaat leassst cooome geeet youuur sss-word." The troll gestured to the rapier beside itself. The sword was lying on the bank, where Jared had dropped it. He looked over at his sister. Her hands were empty too. She must have left her sword at the bottom of the pool.

Mallory took a half-step forward. "That's the only weapon we have."

"Cooome and taaake it. I will clooose my eyeees if it will maake you feeel saaafer." One huge hand covered its eyes.

Mallory looked at the sword in the mud. Her eyes focused on it in a way that made Jared very nervous. She was thinking about trying for it.

"You can't even see the thing," Jared hissed. "Let's go."

"But the sword . . ."

Jared untied the eyepiece and held it out to her. Her face went pale at the sight of the massive creature, peeking through a gap in its fingers, imprisoned only by the fading patches of sunlight.

"Come on," she said shakily.

"Noooo," called the troll. "Cooome baaack. I'll eeeven tuuurn aroooound. I'll cooount to ten. It'll beee a faaair chaaance. Come baaaack."

Jared and Mallory ran on through the woods until they found a patch of sunlight to stop in.

Both leaned against the thick trunk of an oak and tried to catch their breath. Mallory was shivering. Jared didn't know if it was because she was soaked or because of the troll. He unzipped his sweatshirt, took it off, and handed it to her.

"We're lost," Mallory said between gulps of air. "And we're unarmed."

"At least we know they couldn't have crossed the stream," said Jared, struggling to tie the eyepiece back on his head. "The troll would have gotten them for sure."

"But the sound was on the other side." Mallory kicked a tree, chipping off bark.

Jared's nose caught the scent of something burning. It was faint, but he thought it smelled like scorched hair.

"Do you smell that?" Jared asked.

"That way," Mallory said.

They crashed through the brush, heedless of the scratches twigs and thorns made along their arms. Jared's thoughts were all of his brother and fire.

"Look at this." Mallory stopped abruptly. She reached into the grass and picked up a single brown shoe.

"It's Simon's."

"I know," Mallory said. She turned it over, but Jared couldn't see any clues, except that it was muddy.

"You don't think he's . . ." Jared couldn't bring himself to say it.

"No, I don't!" Mallory shoved the shoe in the front pocket of her sweatshirt.

He nodded slowly, allowing himself to be convinced.

A little farther, and the trees began to thin. They stepped out onto a highway. Black

A single brown shoe

asphalt stretched off into the distant horizon. Behind it all, the sun was setting in a blaze of purple and orange.

And on the shoulder of the road, in the distance, a group of goblins huddled around a fire.

Sinister wind chimes

Chapter Five

IN WHICH the Fate of
the Missing Cat Is Discovered

Jared and Mallory approached the goblin camp cautiously, dodging from trunk to trunk. Broken bits of glass and gnawed bones littered the ground. High in the trees they could see cages woven from thornbushes, plastic bags, and other refuse. Squashed soda cans hung from the branches, clattering together like sinister wind chimes.

Ten goblins sat around a fire. The blackened body of something that looked a lot like a cat turned on a stick. Every now and then one

"Skin it raw, skin the fat."

of the goblins would lean over to lick the charred meat, and the goblin turning the spit would bark loudly. Then they would all start barking.

Several of the goblins started to sing. Jared shuddered at the words.

Fidirol, Fidirat!
Catch a dog, catch a cat
Skin it raw, skin the fat
On the spit, turn like that
Fidirol, Fidirat!

Cars whizzed by, oblivious. Perhaps even their mother was driving past now, Jared thought.

"How many?" Mallory whispered, hefting a heavy branch.

"Ten," Jared answered. "I don't see Simon. He must be in one of those cages."

"Are you sure?" Mallory squinted in the direction of the goblins. "Give me that thing."

"Not now," said Jared.

They moved slowly through the trees looking for a cage large enough to contain Simon. Ahead of them, something cried out, shrill and loud. They crept forward to the edge of the forest.

An animal was lying alongside the road, beyond the goblin camp. It was the size of a car, but curled up, with a hawk's head and the body of a lion. Its flank was streaked with blood.

"What do you see?"

"A griffin," said Jared. "It's hurt."

"What's a griffin?"

"It's kind of a bird, kind of a—never mind, just stay away from it."

Mallory sighed, moving deeper into the woods.

"There," she said. "What about those?"

Jared looked up. Several of the high cages were larger, and he thought he could make out a human shape in one of them. Simon!

"I can climb up," Jared said.

Mallory nodded. "Be fast."

Jared wedged his foot in a hollow of the bark, hefting himself up to the first split in the branches. Then, pulling himself higher, he started crawling along the bough that held the little cages. If he stood up on that limb, he would be looking into the cages that were hung higher.

As he edged along, Jared could not help looking down. In the cages below, he could see squirrels, cats, and birds. Some were clawing and biting at the bars, while others were unmoving. A few contained just bones. They were all lined with leaves that looked suspiciously like poison ivy.

"Hey, dribble-puss, over here."

The voice surprised Jared so much he almost lost his grip on the branch. It had come from one of the large cages.

"Who's there?" Jared whispered.

"Hogsqueal. Now how about opening that door?"

Jared saw the frog face of another goblin, but this one had green cat's eyes. It was wearing clothes, and its teeth weren't glass or metal, but what looked like *baby* teeth.

"I don't think so," said Jared. "You can rot in there. I'm not letting you out."

"Don't be a cat-whipper, beetlehead. If I holler, those guys are going to make you into dessert."

"I bet you yell all the time," Jared said. "I bet they don't believe anything you say."

"HEY! LOOK—"

Jared grabbed the edge of the cage and pulled it forward. Hogsqueal went quiet. Below, the goblins slapped one other and snatched pieces of cat meat, apparently unaware of the racket in the tree.

"Okay, okay," Jared said.

"Good. Let me out!" the goblin demanded.

"I have to find my brother. Tell me where he is, and then I'll let you out."

"No way, candy butt. You must think I'm as dumb as a hatful of worms. You let me out or I scream again."

"Jared!" Simon's voice called from one of the cages farther down the branch. "I'm over here."

"I'm coming," Jared called back, turning toward the sound.

"You open this door or I scream," the goblin threatened.

Jared took a deep breath. "You won't scream. If you scream, they'll catch me and then no one's going to let you out. I'm getting my brother out first, but I'll be back for you."

Jared edged farther down the branch. He was relieved that the goblin stayed silent.

Simon was stuffed in a cage much too small for him. His legs were drawn up against his chest, and the toes of one foot stuck through the bars. His bare skin was scraped from the thorns that lined the cage.

"You okay?" Jared asked, taking his pocketknife out and sawing at the knotted

"You okay?"

vines wrapped around Simon's prison.

"I'm fine." Simon's voice quavered just a little.

Jared wanted to ask if Simon had found Tibbs, but he was afraid of the answer. "I'm sorry," he said finally. "I should have helped look for the cat."

"That's okay," said Simon, squeezing out through the part of the door Jared managed to open. "But I have to tell you that —"

"Turtle-head! Boy! Enough mouth! Let me out!" the goblin shouted.

"Come on," said Jared. "I said I'd help him."

Simon followed his twin back along the branch to Hogsqueal's cage.

"What's in there?"

"A goblin, I think."

"A goblin!" Simon exclaimed. "Are you crazy?"

"I can spit in your eye," Hogsqueal offered.

"Gross," said Simon. "No, thanks."

"It will give you the Sight, jinglebrains. Here," Hogsqueal said, taking a handkerchief from one of his pockets and spitting in it. "Rub this on your eyes."

Jared hesitated. Could he trust a goblin? But then, Hogsqueal would be stuck in the cage forever if he did anything bad. Simon would never let the goblin out.

He took off the eyepiece and wiped the dirty cloth over his eyes. It made them sting.

"Ugh. That's the most disgusting thing ever," said Simon.

Jared blinked and looked over at the goblins sitting around their fire. He could see them without the stone. "Simon, it works!"

Simon looked at the cloth skeptically but rubbed his own eyes with goblin spit.

"We had a deal, right? Let me out," Hogsqueal demanded.

"Tell me what you're in there for, first," said Jared. Giving them the handkerchief was nice, but it could still be a trick.

"You're not very chicken-beaked for a nib-head," the goblin grumbled. "I'm in here for letting out one of the cats. See, I like cats, and not just 'cause they're tasty, which they are, no mistake. But they got these eyes that are an awful lot like mine, and this one was real little, not much meat there. And she had this sweet little mewl." The goblin looked lost in his memory, then abruptly looked back at Jared. "So enough about that. Let me out."

"And what about your teeth? Do you eat babies or what?" Jared had not found the goblin's story very reassuring.

"What is this? An interrogation?" Hogsqueal groused.

"I'm letting you out already." Jared came closer and started to cut the complicated knots on the cage. "But I want to know about your teeth."

"Well, kids got this quaint idea of leaving teeth under their pillows, see?"

"You steal kids' teeth?"

"Come on, Dumbellina, tell me you don't believe in the tooth fairy!"

Jared fumbled for a few more moments, saying nothing. He had the last knot almost sawed through when the griffin started screeching.

Four of the goblins circled it with pointed sticks. The animal couldn't seem to raise itself very far off the ground, but it could snap at the goblins if they got too close. Then the creature's hawk beak connected, scissoring off a goblin arm. The wounded goblin squealed while a second drove his stick into the griffin's back. The remaining goblins cheered.

"What are they doing?" Jared whispered.

"What does it look like?" Hogsqueal replied. "They're waiting for it to die."

"They're killing him!" Simon yelled. His eyes were wide, staring down at the gruesome spectacle. Jared realized that his brother was seeing all this for the first time. Suddenly Simon grabbed a handful of leaves and sticks from the tree they were standing on and hurled them at the goblins below.

"Simon, stop it!" Jared said.

"Leave him alone, you jerks!" Simon shouted. "LEAVE HIM ALONE!"

All of the goblins looked up at that moment, their eyes reflecting a ghostly pale white in the dark.

The flames blazed green.

Chapter Six

IN WHICH Jared Is Forced to Make
a Difficult Choice

et me OUT!" Hogsqueal yelled. Jared
snapped into motion and cut through the
last knot.

Hogsqueal danced onto the branch, heedless of the goblins barking beneath him. They
had begun to surround the tree.

Jared looked around for some kind of
weapon, but all he had was his little knife.
Simon was breaking off more branches and
Hogsqueal was running away, jumping from
tree to tree like a monkey. He and his brother

were abandoned and trapped. If they tried to climb down, the goblins would be upon them.

And somewhere down there, in the gloom, Mallory was alone and blind. Her only protection was the red of the sweatshirt she wore.

"What about the animals in the cages?" Simon asked.

"No time!"

"Hey, mucky-pups!" Jared heard Hogsqueal shout. He looked in the direction of the voice, but Hogsqueal wasn't talking to them at all. He was dancing around the campfire and sticking a large strip of burnt cat meat in his mouth.

"Ninnyhammers!" he yelled at the other goblins. "Pestleheads! Goobernuts! Jibbernolls! Fiddlewizzits!" He leaned back and urinated on the fire, making the flames blaze green.

The goblins turned from the tree and headed right for Hogsqueal.

"Move!" Jared said. "Now!"

Simon climbed down the tree as fast as he could, jumping once he was close enough. He fell to the ground with a soft thud. Jared landed beside him.

Mallory hugged them both, but she didn't let go of her stick.

"I heard the goblins get close, but I couldn't see a thing," she said.

"Put this on." Jared held out the eyepiece to her.

"You need it," she protested.

"Now!" Jared said.

Surprisingly Mallory buckled it on without another word. After it was on, she reached into her sweatshirt and gave Simon his shoe.

They started moving into the woods, but Jared couldn't help looking back. Hogsqueal was surrounded like the griffin had been only moments before.

They couldn't leave him like that.

"Hey!" he called. "Over here!"

The goblins turned and, seeing the three children, started moving toward them.

Jared, Mallory, and Simon started to run.

"Are you crazy?" Mallory yelled.

"He was helping us," Jared yelled back. He couldn't be sure she'd heard him since he was panting at the same time he was speaking.

"Where are we going?" Simon shouted.

"The stream," said Jared. He was thinking fast, faster than he'd ever thought in his life. The troll was their only chance. He was sure that it could stop ten goblins with no problem. What he wasn't sure of was how they could avoid it themselves.

"We can't go this way," Mallory said. Jared ignored her.

If only they could jump the stream, maybe

that would be enough. The goblins wouldn't know there was a monster to avoid.

The goblins were still far enough behind. They wouldn't see what was coming.

Almost there. Jared could see the stream ahead, but they weren't to the ruined bridge yet.

Then Jared saw something that stopped him cold. The troll was out of the water. It stood at the edge of the bank, eyes and teeth gleaming in the moonlight. Even hunched over, Jared guessed that it was more than ten feet tall.

"Luckyyyy meee," it said, reaching out a long arm in their direction.

"Wait," said Jared.

The creature moved toward them, a slow smile showing broken teeth. It definitely was not waiting.

"Hear that?" Jared asked. "That's goblins.

It stood at the edge of the bank.

Ten fat goblins. That's a lot more than three skinny kids."

The monster hesitated. The Guide had said that trolls weren't very smart. Jared hoped that was true.

"All you have to do is get back in the stream and we'll lead them right to you. I promise."

The yellow eyes of the creature glinted greedily. "Yesss," it said.

"Hurry!" Jared said. "They're almost here!"

It slid toward the water and dropped under with barely a ripple.

"What was that?" Simon asked.

Jared was shaking, but he could not let that stop him. "Go in the stream there, where it's shallow. We have to get them to chase us through the water."

"Are you nuts?" Mallory demanded.

"Please," Jared begged. "Trust me."

"We have to do something!" said Simon.

"Okay, let's go." Mallory followed her brothers toward the muddy bank, shaking her head.

The goblins burst through the trees. Jared, Mallory, and Simon waded through the shallow water, zigzagging around the pit. The fastest way to go after them would be to cut through the middle of the stream.

Jared heard the goblins splashing behind them, barking madly. Then the barks turned to squeals. Jared looked back to see a few goblins paddling for the shore. The troll grabbed them

all, shaking and biting and dragging them down to his watery lair.

Jared tried not to look any more. His stomach did an odd, nauseous flip-flop.

Simon looked pale and a little queasy.

"Let's go home," Mallory said.

Jared nodded.

"We can't," said Simon. "What about all those animals?"

The full moon overhead

Chapter Seven

IN WHICH Simon Outdoes Himself and Finds an Extraordinary New Pet

"You have to be kidding," Mallory said when Simon explained what he wanted to do.

"They're going to die if we don't," Simon insisted. "The griffin is bleeding."

"The griffin, too?" Jared asked. He understood about the cats, but a griffin?

"How are we going to help that thing?" Mallory demanded. "We're not faerie veterinarians!"

"We have to try," said Simon just as firmly.

Jared owed it to Simon to agree. After all, he had put Simon through a lot. "We could get the old tarp from the carriage house."

"Yeah," Simon chimed in. "Then we could drag the griffin back to the house. There's plenty of room."

Mallory rolled her eyes.

"If it lets us," Jared said. "Did you see what it did to that goblin?"

"Come on, guys," Simon pleaded. "I'm not strong enough to pull it alone."

"All right," she said. "But I'm not standing close to the head."

Jared, Simon, and Mallory trooped back to the carriage house. The full moon overhead gave them enough light to navigate the woods, but they were still careful, crossing the stream where it was barely a trickle. At the edge of the lawn, Jared could see that the windows of the main house were lit and that his mother's car was parked in the gravel driveway. Was she making dinner? Had she called the police? Jared wanted to go inside and tell his mom that they were all okay, but he didn't dare.

"Jared, come on." Simon had opened the door to the carriage house, and Mallory was pulling the tarp from the old car.

"Hey, look at this." Simon picked up a flashlight from one of the shelves and flicked it on. Luckily, no beam of light spread across the lawn.

"Batteries are probably dead," Jared said.

"Stop playing around," Mallory told them. "We're trying *not* to get caught."

They dragged the tarp back through the woods. The walk went more slowly and with a good deal of arguing about the shortest way. Jared couldn't keep from jumping at distant

night noises. Even the croaking of frogs sounded ominous. He couldn't help wondering what else there was, hidden in the dark. Maybe something worse than goblins or trolls. He shook his head and reminded himself that no one could possibly be that unlucky in one day.

When they finally found the goblin camp again, Jared was surprised to see Hogsqueal sitting by the fire. He was licking bones and burped contentedly when they approached.

"I guess you're okay," Jared said.

"Is that any way to talk to someone who saved your prawnheaded hide?"

Jared started to protest—they'd almost gotten killed over the stupid goblin—but Mallory grabbed his arm.

"Help Simon with the animals," she said. "I'll watch the goblin."

"I'm not a goblin," Hogsqueal said. "I'm a *hob*goblin."

"Whatever," said Mallory, sitting on a rock.

Simon and Jared climbed the trees, letting out all the animals in the cages. Most ran down the nearest branch or sprang for the ground, as afraid of the boys as they were of the goblins. One little kitten crouched in the back of a cage, mewling pitifully. Jared didn't know what to do with it, so he put it in his backpack and kept moving. There was no sign of Tibbs.

When Simon saw the kitten, he insisted that they keep it. Jared wished that he meant instead of the griffin.

Jared thought that Hogsqueal's eyes softened when he saw

GRIFFIN

the cat, but that might have been from hunger.

When the cages were empty, the three siblings and the hobgoblin approached the griffin. It watched them warily, extending its claws.

Mallory dropped her end of the tarp. "You know, hurt animals sometimes just attack."

"Sometimes they don't, though," said Simon, walking toward the griffin with open hands. "Sometimes they just let you take care of them. I found a rat like that once. It only bit me when it got better."

"Only a bunch of chuckleheads would mess with a wounded griffin." Hogsqueal cracked open another bone and started sucking out the marrow. "You want me to hold that kitten?"

Mallory scowled at him. "You want to follow your friends to the bottom of the stream?"

Jared smiled. It was good to have Mallory on their side.

That made him think of something. "Since you're feeling so generous, how about a little goblin spit for my sister?"

"It's *hob*goblin spit," Hogsqueal said loftily.

"Gee, thanks," Mallory said, "but I'll pass."

"No, look—it gives you the Sight. And that even makes sense," Jared said. "I mean, if faerie bathwater works, then this should too."

"I can't even begin to express how disgusting those choices are."

"Well, if that's how she feels about it." Hogsqueal was apparently trying to look offended. Jared didn't think he was succeeding at it too well, because he was licking a bone at the same time.

"Mal, come on. You can't wear a stone strapped to your head all the time."

"Says you," she replied. "Do you even know how long this spit is going to last?"

Jared hadn't really considered that. He looked at Hogsqueal.

"Until someone pokes out your eyes," the faerie said.

"Well, then great," Jared said, trying to get back some control of the conversation.

Mallory sighed. "Fine, fine." She knelt

"I'm not going to hurt you."

down and removed the monocle. Hogsqeal spit with great relish.

Looking up, Jared noticed that Simon had already gone over to the griffin. He was squatting down beside it and whispering.

"Hello, griffin," Simon was saying in his most soothing voice. "I'm not going to hurt you. We're just going to help you get better. Come on, be good."

The griffin let out a whine like a kettle's whistle. Simon stroked its feathers lightly.

"Go ahead and spread out the tarp," Simon whispered.

The griffin raised itself slightly, opening its beak, but Simon's petting seemed to relax it. It put its head back down on the asphalt.

They unrolled the tarp behind it.

Simon knelt down by its head, talking softly with cooing words. The griffin appeared to be listening, ruffling its feathers as though Simon's whispers might tickle.

Mallory crept up to one side of it and gently took hold of its front paws, and Jared took hold of the back.

"One, two, three," they said together softly, then rolled the griffin onto the tarp. It squawked and flailed its legs, but by that time it was on the canvas.

Then they lifted it as much as they could and began the arduous process of dragging the griffin to the carriage house. It was lighter than Jared expected. Simon suggested that it might have hollow bones like a bird.

"So long, chidderblains," Hogsqueal called after them.

"See you around," Jared called back. He almost wished the hobgoblin was coming with them.

Mallory rolled her eyes.

The griffin did not enjoy its trip. They couldn't lift it up too far, so it got dragged over bumps and bushes a lot. It screeched and squawked and fluttered its good wing. They had to stop and wait for Simon to calm it down and then start dragging again. It seemed to take forever to get the griffin back home.

Once at the carriage house, they had to open the double doors in the back and haul the griffin into one of the horse stalls. It settled in some of the old straw.

Simon knelt down to clean the griffin's wounds as well as he could by moonlight and with only water from the hose. Jared got a bucket and filled it for the griffin to drink. It gulped gratefully.

Even Mallory pitched in, finding a moth-

At the carriage house

eaten blanket to drape over the animal. It almost looked tame, bandaged and sleepy in the carriage house.

Even though Jared thought it was crazy to bring the griffin back there, he had to admit that he was starting to have a little affection for it. More than he had for Hogsqueal, at any rate.

By the time Jared, Simon, and Mallory limped into the house, it was very late. Mallory was still damp from her fall into the stream, and Simon's clothes were scratched nearly to tatters. Jared had grass stains on his pants and scraped elbows from his chase through the woods. But they still had the book and the eyepiece, and Simon was carrying a kitten the color of butterscotch toffee, and all of them were still alive. From where Jared stood, those things counted as huge successes.

Their mother was on the phone when they came in. Her face was blotchy with tears.

"They're here!" She hung up the phone and stared at them for a moment. "Where were you? It is one o'clock in the morning!" She pointed her finger at Mallory. "How could you be so irresponsible?"

Mallory looked over at Jared. Simon, on his other side, looked at him too and clutched the cat to his chest. It suddenly occurred to Jared that they were waiting for him to come up with an excuse.

"Um . . . there was a cat in a tree," Jared started. Simon gave him an encouraging smile. "That cat." Jared indicated the kitten in Simon's arms. "And, you see, Simon climbed up the tree, but the kitten got scared. It climbed up even farther and Simon got stuck. And I ran back and got Mallory."

"And I tried to climb after him," Mallory offered.

"Right," Jared said. "She climbed after him. And then the cat jumped into another tree and Simon climbed after it, but the branch broke and he fell in a stream."

"But his clothes aren't wet," their mother said, scowling.

"Jared means that *I* fell in the stream," Mallory said.

"And my *shoe* fell in the stream," said Simon.

"Yeah," Jared said. "Then Simon caught the cat, but then we had to get them out of the tree without him getting clawed up."

"It took a while," said Simon.

Their mother gave Jared a strange look, but she didn't yell. "You three are grounded for the rest of the month. No playing outside and no more excuses."

Jared opened his mouth to argue, but he

couldn't think of a single thing to say.

As the three of them trooped up the stairs, Jared said, "I'm sorry. I guess that was a pretty pathetic excuse."

Mallory shook her head. "There wasn't much you could say. You couldn't explain what really happened."

"Where did those goblins come from?" Jared asked. "We never even found out what they wanted."

"The Guide," Simon said. "That's what I started to tell you before. They thought I had it."

"But how? How could they know that we found it?"

"You don't think that Thimbletack would have told them, do you?" Mallory asked.

Jared shook his head. "He didn't want us to mess with the book in the first place."

Mallory sighed. "Then how?"

"What if someone was watching the house, waiting for us to find the book?"

"Someone or something," Simon added worriedly.

"But why?" Jared asked a little louder than he intended. "What's so important about the book? I mean—could those goblins even read?"

Simon shrugged. "They didn't really say why. They just wanted it."

"Thimbletack was right." Jared opened the door to the room he shared with his twin.

Simon's bed was neatly made, the sheets pulled back and the pillow plumped. But Jared's bed was ruined. The mattress hung from the frame, strewn with feathers and stuffing. The sheets had been ripped to ribbons.

"Thimbletack!" said Jared.

"I told you," said Mallory. "You should never have grabbed that stone."

End of
BOOK TWO

About TONY DiTERLIZZI . . .

A *New York Times* best-selling author, Tony DiTerlizzi created the Zena Sutherland Award–winning *Ted*, *Jimmy Zangwow's Out-of-This-World Moon Pie Adventure*, as well as illustrations in Tony Johnson's Alien and Possum beginning-reader series. Most recently, his brilliantly cinematic version of Mary Howitt's classic *The Spider and the Fly* was awarded a Caldecott Honor. In addition, Tony's art has graced the work of such well-known fantasy names as J.R.R. Tolkien, Anne McCaffrey, Peter S. Beagle, and Greg Bear as well as Wizards of the Coast's *Magic The Gathering*. He and his wife, Angela, reside with their pug, Goblin, in Amherst, Massachusetts. Visit Tony on the World Wide Web at www.diterlizzi.com.

and HOLLY BLACK

An avid collector of rare folklore volumes, Holly Black spent her early years in a decaying Victorian mansion where her mother fed her a steady diet of ghost stories and books about faeries. Accordingly, her first novel, *Tithe: A Modern Faerie Tale,* is a gothic and artful glimpse at the world of Faerie. Published in the fall of 2002, it received two starred reviews and a Best Book for Young Adults citation from the American Library Association. She lives in West Long Branch, New Jersey, with her husband, Theo, and a remarkable menagerie. Visit Holly on the World Wide Web at www.blackholly.com.

Tony and Holly continue to work day and night fending off angry faeries and goblins in order to bring the Grace children's story to you.

ACKNOWLEDGMENTS

Tony and Holly would like to thank
Steve and Dianna for their insight,
Starr for her honesty,
Myles and Liza for sharing the journey,
Ellen and Julie for helping make this our reality,
Kevin for his tireless enthusiasm and faith in us,
and especially Angela and Theo—
there are not enough superlatives
to describe your patience
in enduring endless nights
of Spiderwick discussion.

The text type for this book is set in Cochin.
The display types are set in Nevins Hand and Rackham.
The illustrations are rendered in pen and ink.